DATE DUE

DEC 2 2			

Library Store #47-0108 Peel Off Pressure Sensitive

EXPERIMENTS
with
PHYSICAL SCIENCE

Zella Williams

PowerKiDS press™

New York

Published in 2007 by The Rosen Publishing Group, Inc.
29 East 21st Street, New York, NY 10010

First Edition

Editor: Joanne Randolph
Book Design: Greg Tucker and Ginny Chu
Photo Researcher: Sam Cha

Photo Credits: Cover © Photodisc/Punchstock; p. 5 © shutterstock; pp. 6, 7, 18, 19, 20, 21 © Adriana Skura; pp. 8, 9, 10, 11 © Scott Bauer; pp. 12, 13 © Shalhevet Moshe; pp. 14, 15, 16, 17 © Cindy Reiman.

Library of Congress Cataloging-in-Publication Data

Williams, Zella.
  Experiments with physical science / Zella Williams. — 1st ed.
      p. cm. — (Do-it-yourself science)
  Includes index.
  ISBN-13: 978-1-4042-3659-2 (library binding)
  ISBN-10: 1-4042-3659-7 (library binding)
  1. Physics—Experiments—Juvenile literature. 2. Physics projects—Juvenile literature. I. Title.
  QC26.W56 2007
  530.078—dc22
                                        2006024095

Manufactured in the United States of America

Contents

What Is Physical Science?

Physical science is the study of **energy**, nonliving matter, and the workings of the natural world. From light, sound, and **electricity** to **magnetism** and **gravity**, physical science tells you how everything around you works!

Have you wondered why the sky is blue? Have you wondered what makes a ball fall to the ground when you drop it? **Scientists** do **experiments** to find out the answers to their questions. You can do some physical science experiments, too.

Lightning is electricity. Lightning strikes somewhere on Earth about 100 times every second.

Sound on the Move

Did you know that sound moves? That is how it makes it from your mouth to your friend's ears. Sound does not move in a **straight** line, though. It moves in waves, like the ones you see ocean water make at the beach. Sound waves travel through the air in all directions. Follow these steps to get an idea of how sound waves work.

You will need

- a large bowl
- water
- food coloring
- small stones

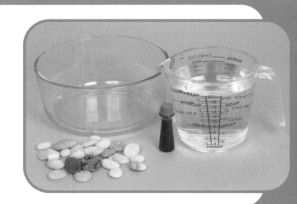

1 Fill a bathtub, kitchen sink, or a dishpan with water.

2 Add a few drops of food coloring.

3

4

Drop a small stone into the water. What do you see? Ring-shaped waves travel out in all directions.

Try dropping two stones in the water at the same time but in different places. Two stones make two sets of waves that pass through each other. Sound waves move in the same way. That's why you can hear several different kinds of sound at one time.

Sound You Can See

Sound is a kind of energy. As the energy reaches your ear, it causes your eardrum to vibrate. "To vibrate" means "to move back and forth quickly." Your eardrum is a thin, tight **membrane**. In this experiment you will see how different sounds cause a thin membrane, like your eardrum, to move in different ways.

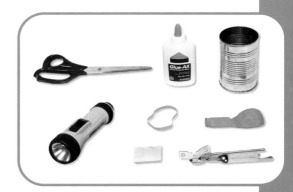

You will need

- a coffee can
- a can opener
- scissors
- a balloon
- a large rubber band
- a small mirror
- glue
- a flashlight

8

1 Ask an adult to help you remove both ends of a coffee can with a can opener. The ends will be sharp, so handle them carefully.

2 Cut the neck off of a balloon with scissors. Pull the balloon over one end of the coffee can. Make sure that it is pulled tightly over the end of the can. Keep the balloon in place with a rubber band.

3 Glue a mirror to the balloon. After the glue has dried, lay the can on its side on a table in a darkened room.

4 Lay a flashlight on the table so that it shines on the mirror at about a **45-degree angle**. Move the can and the flashlight as needed so that the light coming from the mirror shines on a white wall.

5 Yell into the open end of the coffee can. What happens to the light? What is the softest sound that you can "see" using your coffee can sound viewer?

The Color of Light

Light is energy. Light doesn't seem to have much color, but it is made up of all the colors of the rainbow. In fact, a rainbow happens when drops of water in the sky break up all the colors that make up white light. In this experiment you will break white light into its many colors.

You will need

- a shallow pan
- a small mirror
- a clipboard
- a pencil
- a strong flashlight
- balloons
- white paper
- water

1 Fill a pan with water and place it in direct sunlight.

2 Place a mirror in the water at an angle facing the Sun.

3 Wait until the water becomes still and hold up a sheet of paper on a clipboard. Move it around until you see the rainbow of colors.

4 Write down the order of the colors as they appear on the paper.

5 Now try the experiment again in a darkened room using a strong flashlight. Are the colors in the same order? Try changing the color of the light from the flashlight beam by pulling different-colored balloons tightly over the end of the flashlight. What happens?

Which do you think would move faster down a slide, a bowling ball or a tennis ball? The bowling ball would move faster because it is heavier. The way something picks up **speed** once it is moving is called **acceleration**. Weight changes acceleration. **Friction** changes acceleration, too. Friction slows things down. Try this.

You will need

- 2 small toy cars
- a roll of masking tape

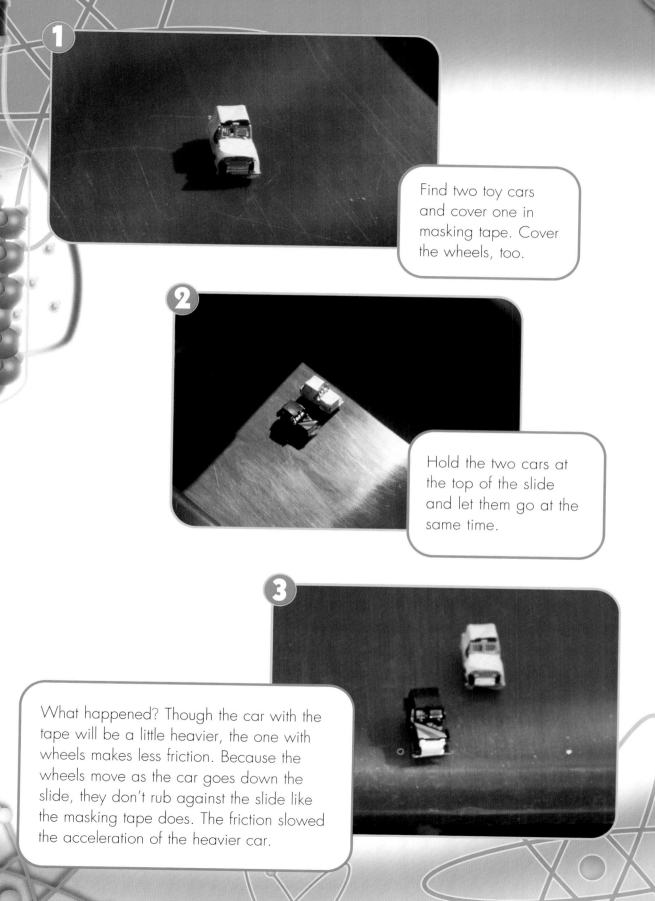

1

Find two toy cars and cover one in masking tape. Cover the wheels, too.

2

Hold the two cars at the top of the slide and let them go at the same time.

3

What happened? Though the car with the tape will be a little heavier, the one with wheels makes less friction. Because the wheels move as the car goes down the slide, they don't rub against the slide like the masking tape does. The friction slowed the acceleration of the heavier car.

That's Magnetic!

You have likely seen magnets on your refrigerator. Have you ever thought about how they work, though? Magnets have the power to pull things close or to push them away. They push things with a like force away. They pull things with an opposite, or unlike, force toward them. Try this to see magnetism in action.

You will need

- 2 bar magnets
- tape
- a toy car

1 Tape a bar magnet to the top of a small toy car.

2 Hold another bar magnet near the car.

3

You can make the car move away from you by pointing one end of the bar magnet toward the car. To make the car move toward you, point the other end of the magnet toward the car.

4 What happened? Each magnet has two **poles**, a north pole and a south pole. If you put two north poles near each other, they will push away from each other. If you put a north pole and a south pole near each other, they will pull together.

Make an Electromagnet

Some magnets keep their magnetic force for a long time. Other magnets can be turned on and off. Electricity can be used to make magnets that can be turned on and off. These magnets are called electromagnets. Electromagnets are found in many things, such as doorbells, telephones, and washing machines. You can make an electromagnet.

You will need

- wire
- a yardstick
- a long iron nail
- a 6-volt battery
- scissors
- metallic and nonmetallic things

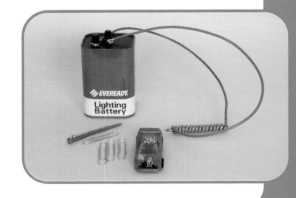

1 Use a yardstick to measure 2 to 3 feet (61–91 cm) of plastic-coated wire.

2 Have an adult help you cut away about ½ inch (1.3 cm) of plastic at each end to get at the wire.

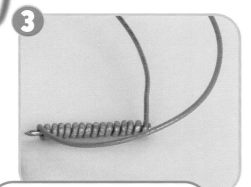

3 Tightly wind the wire around a long iron nail. The more times you wind the wire around the nail, the stronger your electromagnet will be.

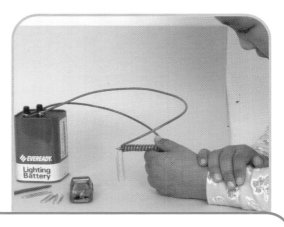

4 Fix the ends of the wire to a **battery**. See how many things you can pick up by using your electromagnet. What kinds of things can your magnet pick up?

Gravity Games

Gravity works a little bit like a magnet. When you jump into the air, you don't keep going up forever. You quickly get pulled back to Earth. This is because of gravity's pull. You can see the force of gravity in action during many games that you play. Try this.

You will need

- 2 balls of equal size

1 Watch two friends toss a ball back and forth to each other. Watch the path of the ball in the air carefully.

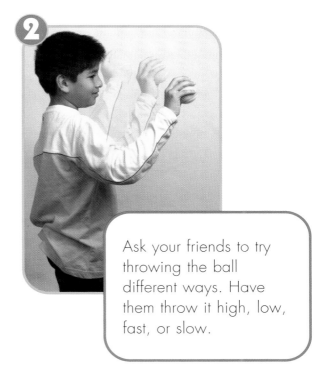

2 Ask your friends to try throwing the ball different ways. Have them throw it high, low, fast, or slow.

3 What happens? No matter how your friends throw the ball, the path of the ball is the same while it is in the air. The ball goes up when it's thrown, and then it comes back down. That's the force of gravity!

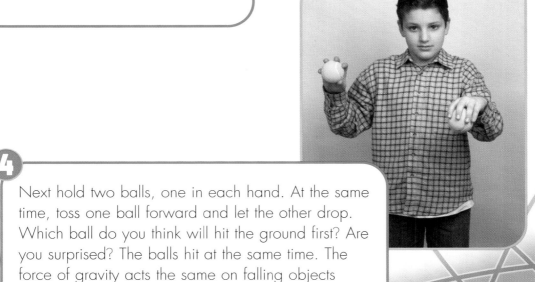

4 Next hold two balls, one in each hand. At the same time, toss one ball forward and let the other drop. Which ball do you think will hit the ground first? Are you surprised? The balls hit at the same time. The force of gravity acts the same on falling objects whether they are moving forward or straight down.

Gravity Works!

Gravity can be put to work in many ways. Gravity pulls water over a mountain edge to make a waterfall. This waterfall can be used to turn a waterwheel in a power station to make electricity. We use electricity to give us light and for many other things. Let's make a waterwheel and put gravity to work!

You will need

- a plastic soda or juice bottle
- a cork
- scissors
- a large nail
- toothpicks
- clay
- a small potato
- rubber tubing
- colored water
- a funnel
- tape
- a sheet of stiff plastic
- a bowl

1

Have an adult cut off the bottom of a plastic soda or juice bottle. Then ask the adult to poke holes in opposite sides of the bottle with a large nail.

2

Next make the paddles for your waterwheel. Cut a sheet of hard plastic into four pieces that are ½ inch wide by 2 ½ inches long (1.3 x 6.4 cm). Make four thin, evenly spaced cuts on the sides of a cork. Slide the plastic pieces into the cuts you have made.

3

Push a toothpick into one end of the cork. Place the cork into the bottle so that the toothpick fits through one hole. Push a toothpick through the other hole and into the other end of the cork. Put clay at the ends of each toothpick.

4

Stand the bottle up in a bowl. Use strong tape to fix one end of some rubber tube to the bottom of a **funnel**. Tape the other end of the tube to the mouth of the bottle.

5

Holding the funnel high, dump colored water into the funnel and the tube. Watch gravity power your waterwheel.

21

Fun with Physical Science

You have now done a group of physical science experiments. Isn't physical science fun? When you see a rainbow or play catch with your friends, you can share what you know about light or gravity. Can you think of other ways to use what you have learned in these experiments?

Keep asking questions and think of ways to find out the answers. You can be a physical scientist each and every day!

Glossary

acceleration (ik-SEH-luh-ray-shun) How much faster something moves once it starts moving.

battery (BA-tuh-ree) A thing in which energy, or power, is stored.

electricity (ih-lek-TRIH-suh-tee) Power that produces light, heat, or movement.

energy (EH-ner-jee) The power to do work.

experiments (ek-SPER-uh-ments) A set of actions or steps taken to learn more about something.

45-degree angle (for-tee-FYV-dih-gree AYN-gul) One-eighth of a circle.

friction (FRIK-shin) The rubbing of one thing against another.

funnel (FUH-nul) A tool that is wide at the top and narrow at the bottom.

gravity (GRA-vih-tee) The natural force that causes things to move toward the center of Earth.

magnetism (MAG-nuh-tih-zum) The force that pulls certain things toward one another.

membrane (MEM-brayn) A soft, thin bit of living matter that comes from a plant or an animal.

poles (POHLZ) The parts of a magnet where the force of magnetism is strongest.

scientists (SY-un-tists) People who study the world by using experiments.

speed (SPEED) How quickly something moves.

straight (STRAYT) Direct or without bend.

Index

A

acceleration, 12–13
answers, 4, 22

B

ball(s), 4, 12, 19
battery, 17

E

electricity, 4, 16, 20
energy, 4, 8, 10
experiment(s), 4, 8,
    10–11, 22

F

45-degree angle, 9
friction, 12–13
funnel, 21

G

gravity, 4, 18–22
ground, 4, 19

L

light, 4, 9, 10–11, 22

M

magnetism, 4, 14
membrane, 8

P

poles, 15

S

scientist(s), 4, 22
sky, 4, 10
sound, 4, 6–9
speed, 12

W

water, 6–7, 10–11. 20–21
waves, 6–7

Web Sites

Due to the changing nature of Internet links, PowerKids Press has developed an online list of Web sites related to the subject of this book. This site is updated regularly. Please use this link to access the list:
www.powerkidslinks.com/diysci/physci/